Happy first
Birthday Kate!


Love,
The Rockfellers

# No Peas for Nellie

# No Peas for Nellie

Story and pictures by Chris L. Demarest

Macmillan Publishing Company   New York

*For Joey*

Printed and bound by South China Printing Company, Hong Kong. First American Edition    10    9    8    7    6    5    4    3    2    1

The text of this book is set in 18 point ITC Zapf International Light. The illustrations are rendered in watercolor and pen-and-ink.
*Library of Congress Cataloging-in-Publication Data*    Demarest, Chris L. No peas for Nellie.    Summary: Nellie imagines all the things she would rather eat than her peas, and while doing so she finishes them all.    [1. Peas – Fiction] I. Title. PZ7.D3914No    1988      [E]      87-14167
ISBN 0-02-728460-3

Nellie doesn't like peas.

"Peas are good for you," her mother said at dinner.
"Try them one at a time."
"No. No peas," said Nellie. "I don't like them."

"No peas, no dessert," said her father.
"Well, then, maybe just one," said Nellie.
"But there are other things I'd rather eat.

I'd rather eat

a big, furry spider

or a wet, slimy salamander.

I'd have a big helping

of hairy warthog,

followed by
a pair of aardvarks

and a python.

Now, that would be good. YUM!

I'd even rather eat

a big, old crocodile

or a water buffalo—

with salt and pepper, of course.

And watch out, Mr. Lion.
I'm not through yet. ROAR!

No pea could be as tasty
as a serving of giraffe.

And then an elephant, trunk and all—

Yes, that would be perfect. DELICIOUS!"

Nellie sat back and smiled.

"Those are the things I'd rather eat."

"Thank you, Nellie, for eating all your peas," said her mother.

"Now would you please finish your milk?"
said her father.